THIS BOOK BELONGS TO:

For my mum, who makes Christmas - L.C.

For my beautiful cousins, Vikki & Vanessa x - N.D.

ORCHARD BOOKS
First published in Great Britain in 2019 by The Watts Publishing Group

2 4 6 8 10 9 7 5 3 1

Text © Lou Carter, 2019 • Illustrations © Nikki Dyson, 2019

ISBN HB 978 1 40835 581 7 PB 978 1 40835 582 4
Printed and bound in China

IMPORTANT INFORMATION:
DO NOT EAT!

FSC
www.fsc.org

MIX
Paper from
responsible sources
FSC® C104740

Orchard Books, an imprint of Hachette Children's Group
Part of The Watts Publishing Group Limited
Carmelite House, 50 Victoria Embankment
London EC4Y 0DZ

An Hachette UK Company
www.hachette.co.uk

www.hachettechildrens.co.uk

Oscar

the Hungry Unicorn **EATs CHRISTMAS**

Lou Carter

ORCHARD

Nikki Dyson

It's Christmas Eve and nobody can sleep.

Princess Oola is

TOO EXCITED...

GASP!

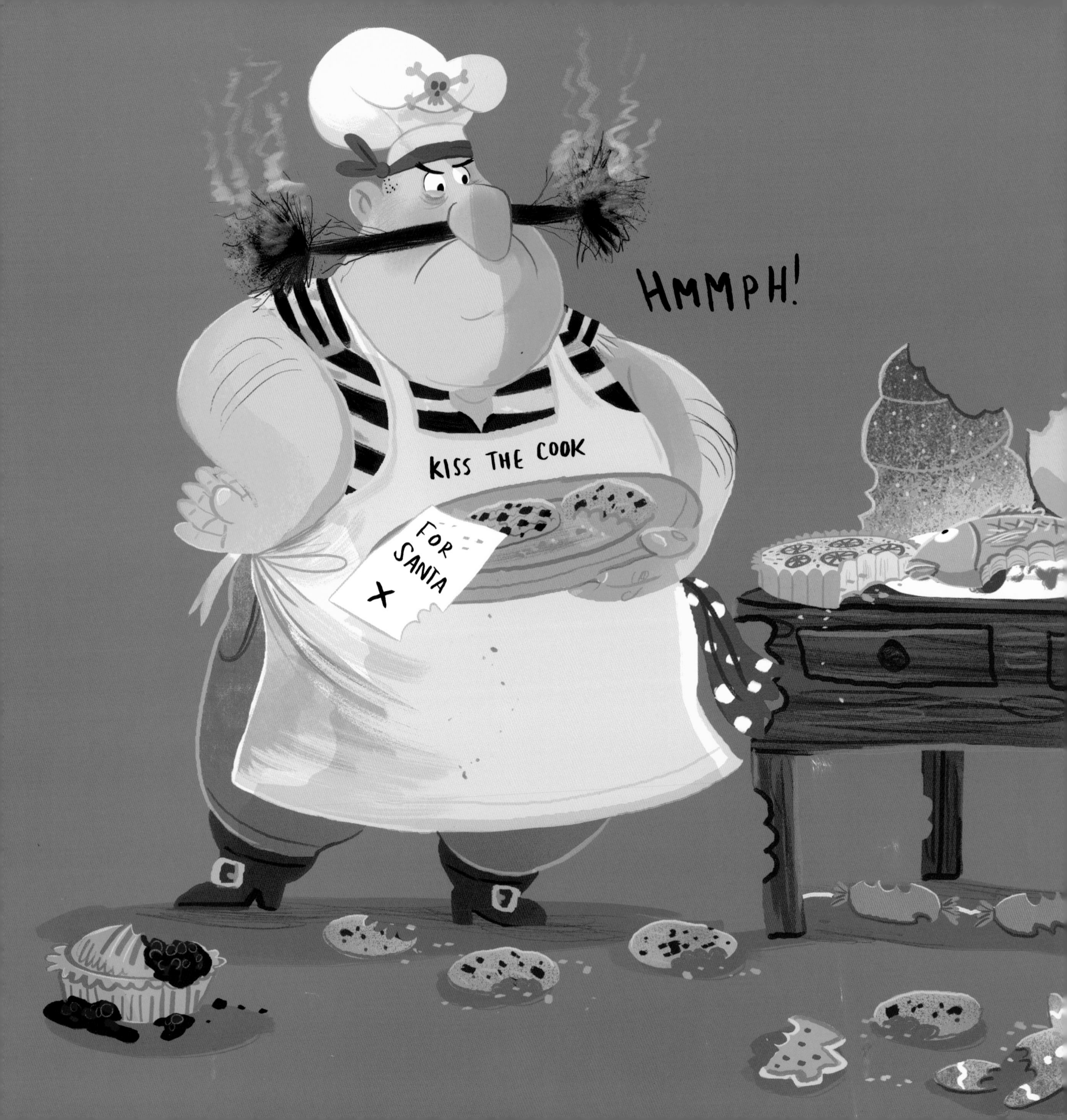
HMMPH!
KISS THE COOK
FOR SANTA
X

...and Oscar the Unicorn is TOO HUNGRY.
(OSCAR IS ALWAYS HUNGRY.)

MUNCH MUNCH

The king won't be pleased
that Oscar has eaten the
STOCKINGS.
(THE STRIPY ONES ARE HIS FAVOURITES.)

The fairy doesn't like Oscar
eating her **TREE.**

(Oola **IS** always telling Oscar to eat his greens.)

MUNCH
MUNCH

And Santa isn't happy that Oscar has eaten the

PRESENTS.

(Not the bows though. They get stuck in his teeth.)

Hmph

There is still a long way to travel tonight.
Santa ought to get a move on.

But wait a minute . . .

Santa says it's **NOT** and writes Oscar's name on a list.
Without their food, the reindeer won't be able to fly.
And Santa won't be able to deliver the presents.

But Oola has an idea . . .

WHOOSH!

HUH!?

SWOOSH!

Oscar will be the amazingest

REINDICORN

ever, she says.

The Magic Reindeer Food
works a treat. Oscar has
never moved so fast ...

. . . and Santa has never delivered
the presents so quickly.

They're back at the
North Pole in record time.

(THE ELVES WEREN'T EXPECTING SANTA HOME JUST YET!)

SWOOSH!

NORTH POLE →

★ NORTH POLE ★
Magic Reindeer
FOOD

Oscar likes the North Pole.
There's **LOTS** to eat.
(Not Santa's pants though,
Mrs Claus says.)

PING!

But Oola says they must get back to the castle. Otherwise they'll miss Christmas.

There's just time for a quick nap before morning.
No peeking at the presents, Oola says. (Or nibbling.)

Christmas morning is full of surprises!

(AND OSCAR LOVES HIS STOCKING.)

Oscar has saved Christmas for
EVERYONE, Oola says.

(WELL, ALMOST EVERYONE.)

SHIVER
SHIVER